289606

P1-3

F

The ure
book ing.
There use,
a da
with
an e
lots
of n:

F
BAR

Falkirk Council

T
an d.

TEE HEE!

HA HA!

For Lucy and David

First published 1996 by Walker Books Ltd
87 Vauxhall Walk, London SE11 5HJ
This edition published 1997
2 3 4 5 6 7 8 9 10
© 1996 Alan Baron
This book has been typeset in Veronan.
Printed in Hong Kong
British Library Cataloguing in Publication Data
A catalogue record for this book is
available from the British Library.
ISBN 0-7445-5280-X

Little Pig's Bouncy Ball

ALAN BARON

WALKER BOOKS
AND SUBSIDIARIES
LONDON · BOSTON · SYDNEY

Little Pig was playing with her ball.
"Here, kick it to me!" said Dan Dog.
The ball bounced over Dan Dog's head.
Dan Dog ran after it.

Little Pig waited.
Dan Dog didn't come back.
Along came Tabby Cat.
"Dan Dog's run away with my ball,"
said Little Pig.
Little Pig started to cry.
Tabby Cat gave her a hug.

Along came Fat Hen.
"Dan Dog's run away
with Little Pig's ball,"
said Tabby Cat.
Tabby Cat started to cry.
Little Pig bawled.
Fat Hen gave them both a hug.

Along came Big Duck and Lucy Goose.
"Dan Dog's run away with
Little Pig's ball," said Fat Hen.
Fat Hen started to cry.
Tabby Cat bawled.
Little Pig screamed.
Big Duck and Lucy Goose hugged them all,
then they started to cry as well.

So there they all were –
crying and bawling and screaming
because Dan Dog ran away
with Little Pig's ball.

Then to everyone's surprise,
Dan Dog came back.
"Phew! What a bouncy, bouncy ball!"
said Dan Dog. "I had to run miles
to fetch it."
For a moment, no one knew what to say...

Then Little Pig,
Tabby Cat, Fat Hen,
Big Duck and Lucy Goose
all fell in a heap, laughing!

"Here, kick it to me," said Little Pig.
The ball bounced over Little Pig's head.
Little Pig, Tabby Cat, Fat Hen,
Big Duck and Lucy Goose ran after it.
Bounce bounce, down the hill
and far away.

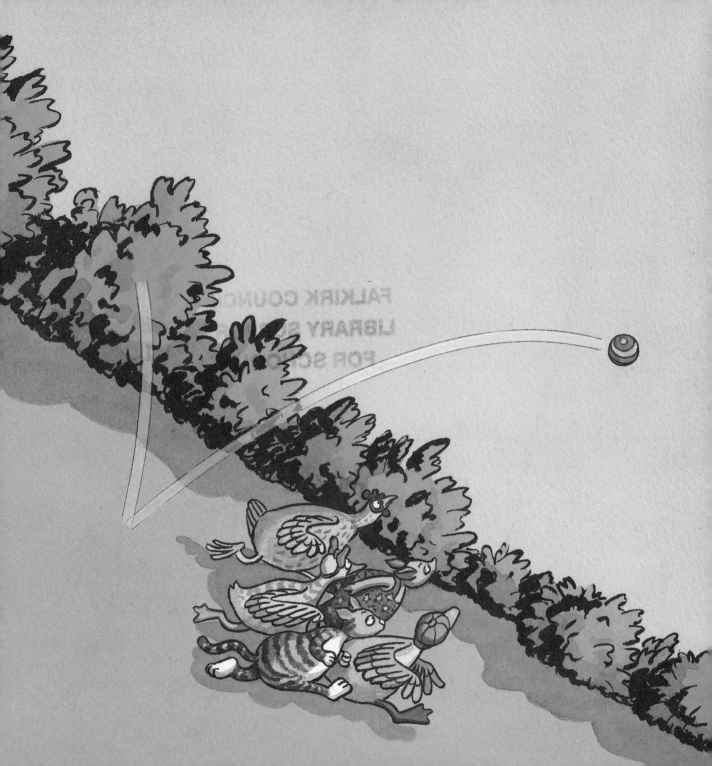